WELCOME TO MY NEIGHBORHOOD!

A BARRIO A·B·C

by **Quiara Alegría Hudes**

illustrated by **Shino Arihara**

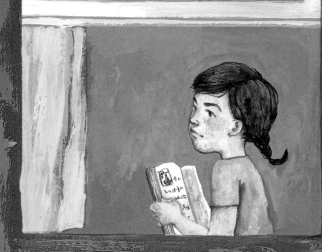

ARTHUR A. LEVINE BOOKS
AN IMPRINT OF SCHOLASTIC INC.

For Cecilia
–Q. A. H.

For Ken
–S. A.

A is for *abuela*.

And abandoned car.

B is for the bottles
     that are smashed like falling stars.
Broken bottles of black cherry soda
               bought at barrio bodegas.

C is for the Chino-Latino
corner store we call Ortega's.

D is for dominoes. *Abuela* taught me to play.
Double six dominoes during summer days.

E is for the echo of the elevated train.

F is for the fire hydrant spraying summer rain.

G is for graffiti right
beside the subway grate.

H is for the hoop.
It used to be a plastic crate.

I is for the ice-cream truck in infinite flavors so sweet.

J is for *los jíbaros* jamming in the jungle of concrete.

K is for the kitchen window where kidney beans boil and pork chops pop.

L is for the living room ledges and little old ladies who guard the block.

M is for *los muralistas*, making murals of island vistas.
Waterfalls that hide brick walls. Rain forests full of tropical trees.

N is for the noisy neighbors who sit
on the stoop and catch the breeze.

O is for Ontario,
a tiny street where
cars can't squeeze.

P for Porky's Point, my papi's favorite roast pig joint.

Q is for *quemar*, to burn a house to the ground beneath, making a block full of row homes look like a smile that's missing its two front teeth.

R for mami's favorite word.
She always says, "Remember.
Remember that, remember when,
remember all the things now gone!
Remember red-comb roosters
singing *qui-qui-ri-qui* to the dawn!
Remember Rincón Beach in Puerto Rico,
how the sun would set!"

S for all the Spanish words
I somehow still forget!

T is for the trolley tracks.
One set goes forward,
one set goes back.

U is for a universe of maple roots and sidewalk cracks.

V is for the vegetable plot that used to be a vacant lot.

W is for wise.

X is for XXL, my
favorite T-shirt size.

Y is for yams and yuca
planted by my cousin Cuca.

Z Street's loud with zooming cars.
(They speed right through the crosswalk bars.)

Abuela's making ham and cheese.
I'll race you home! It's not too far!

Text copyright © 2010 by Quiara Alegría Hudes · Illustrations copyright © 2010 by Shino Arihara

All rights reserved. Published by Arthur A. Levine Books, an imprint of Scholastic Inc., *Publishers since 1920*.
SCHOLASTIC and the LANTERN LOGO are trademarks and/or registered trademarks of Scholastic Inc.

Library of Congress Cataloging-in-Publication Data

Hudes, Quiara Alegría.
Welcome to my neighborhood! : a barrio ABC / by Quiara Alegría Hudes ; illustrated by Shino Arihara. — 1st ed.   p. cm.
Summary: A young girl takes a walk through her urban neighborhood, observing items representing every letter of the alphabet, from her abuela to loud, zooming cars.
ISBN 978-0-545-09424-5 (hardcover : alk. paper)
[1. Stories in rhyme. 2. Neighborhoods—Fiction. 3. City and town life—Fiction. 4. Hispanic Americans—Fiction. 5. Alphabet.] I. Arihara, Shino, 1973- ill. II. Title.
PZ8.3.H8557Wel 2010   [E]—dc22   2009049818
10 9 8 7 6 5 4 3 2 1   10 11 12 13 14

Book design by Lillie Howard

First edition, August 2010

Printed in Singapore   46

The art for this book was created using gouache.